*

Perplexed

By

J.J. BHATT

ISBN:

9798850103835

Title:

Perplexed

Author:

J.J. Bhatt

Published and Distributed by Amazon and
Kindle worldwide.

This book is manufactured in the Unites States of America.

Recent Books by J.J. Bhatt

HUMAN ENDEAVOR: *Essence & Mission/ A Call for Global Awakening, (*2011)

ROLLING SPIRITS: *Being Becoming* /A Trilogy, (2012)

ODYSSEY OF THE DAMNED: *A Revolving Destiny,* (2013).

PARISHRAM: *Journey of the Human Spirits*, (2014).

TRIUMPH OF THE BOLD: *A Poetic Reality*, (2015).

THEATER OF WISDOM, (*2016).*

MAGNIFICENT QUEST: *Life, Death & Eternity,* (2016).

ESSENCE OF INDIA: *A Comprehensive Perspective,* (2016).

ESSENCE OF CHINA: *Challenges & Possibilities*, (2016).

BEING & MORAL PERSUASION: *A Bolt of Inspiration*, (2017).

REFELCTIONS, RECOLLECTIONS & EXPRESSIONS, (2018).

ONE, TWO, THREE... ETERNITY: *A Poetic Odyssey, (*2018).

INDIA: *Journey of Enlightenment*, (2019a).

SPINNING MIND, SPINNING TIME: *C'est la vie*, (2019b).Book 1.

MEDITATION ON HOLY TRINITY, *(2019c),* Book 2.

ENLIGHTENMENT: *Fiat lux*, (2019d), Book 3.

BEING IN THE CONTEXTUAL ORBIT: *Rhythm, Melody & Meaning, (*2019e).

QUINTESSENCE: *Thought & Action,* (2019f).

THE WILL TO ASCENT: *Power of Boldness & Genius,* (2019g).

RIDE ON A SPINNING WHEEL: *Existence Introspected, (*2020a).

A FLASH OF LIGHT: *Splendors, Perplexities & Riddles,* (2020b).

ON A ZIG ZAG TRAIL: *The Flow of Life*, (2020c).

UNBOUNDED: *An Inner Sense of Destiny* (2020d).

REVERBERATIONS: The *Cosmic Pulse,* (2020e).

LIGHT & DARK: *Dialogue and Meaning,* (2021a).

ROLLING REALITY: *Being in flux, (2021b).*

FORMAL SPLENDOR: *The Inner Rigor,* (2021c).

TEMPORAL TO ETERNAL: *Unknown Expedition,* (2021d).

TRAILBLAZERS: *Spears of Courage*, (2021e).

TRIALS & ERRORS: *A Path to Human Understanding*, (2021f).

MEASURE OF HUMAN EXPERIENCE: *Brief Notes,* (2021g).

LIFE: *An Ellipsis (2022a).*

VALIDATION: *The Inner Realm of Essence* (2022b).

LET'S ROLL: *Brave Heart,* (2022c).

BEING BECOMING, (2022d).

INVINCIBLE, (2022e)/ THE CODE: *DESTINY,* (2022f).

LIFE DIMYSTIFIED, (2022g) / ESSENTIAL HUMANITY, (2022h).

MORAL ADVENTURE, (2022i / SPIRALING SPHERES (2022h).
EPHEMERAL SPLENDOR, (2023a / CHAOTIC *HARMONY,* (2023b).
Intellectual Mysticism (2023c) / *Will to Believe* (2023d)
Expectations & Reality, (2023e) / *Thread That Binds* (2023f).
Once & Forever, *(2023g) /* **Perplexed**, *(2023h).*

PREFACE

Perplexed affirms life per se is an amazing bewilderment. It is time; we understand the limitations and scope of our contradictions, paradoxes and riddles while concomitantly looking for clarity of the reality where we are the scintillating sparks of it. Let us, journey together through the following pages to get some grip over, "Where are we heading?"

J.J. Bhatt

CONTENT

Preface................... 5
Perplexed.............. 11
Be Calm 12
Recurrences............13
The Way............... 14
Existence 101......... 15
Reflection 16
Light & Shadow... 17
Nova Prayer 18
Endurance 19
Introspection 20
Believe it 21
Inspiration 22
Our Time............ 23
First Cause 24
Image 25
Precious 26
Forever 27
Sweetie 28
Great March 29
Queries............. 30
Sinners 31
Imitators 32
Revival 33
Not Singing........ 34
Fortitude 35
Amnesia 36
Explorer........... 37
Cosmic Puzzle.... 38

When it Rains............ 39
Being & Identity........ 40
Mission To Be 41
Leap of Self-faith....... 42
The Spirit 43
Epiphany 44
Obsolescent 45
Perfection 46
Beware 47
Juggernaut 48
Road to Clarity 49
Scope & Limits 50
Until Forever............ 51
Be Bold 52
Point Upward.......... . 53
Roll the Ball 54
Gardeners............... 55
Noble Warriors 56
Synergy 57
Mystical Flow 58
Being & Existence....... .59
Time Travelers 60
Will to Win 61
Rise Above.................. 62
Essence & 63
Connectivity 64
Journeymen 65
Great Walk 66
Being & Reality......... . 67

7

Conundrum 68
In This Age 69
Falling in Love......... 70
Ascending Thrust...... 71
Liberation 72
A Point 73
Short Falls 74
Universal Human 75
Odd Balls............... 76
As Ever 77
First Principle 78
Note Well 79
Illumined 80

Noble Journey 81
Fearless 82
Reckoning 83
Perplexity 84
Flush it out 85
Reciprocity 86
Wind of Change... 87
Dice is cast 88
Be Alert 89
Moral Will............ 90
The Path 91
The Quest 92
Jet Stream 93
Arrows In-flight..... 94

Outcome............ 95
Not quite........... 96
I Dare 97
Unsettled 98
Biggest Gamble.... . 99
Epicenter 100
Happy Morons.... 101
Closing Curtain... 102
Flickers 103
Rhythms........... 104
Mistaken 105
Being & 106
A Spin .... .107
Line in the 108
Return 109
We're 110
Blind Logic 111
Smart Idiots...... 112
Here & Now..... 113
Gear-up 114
Perfunctory 115
Keep Walking.... 116
Through Time... 117
Let's Fly off...... 118
An Epic............ 119
Dots of 120
Being &......... 121
Life Force....... 122

Clarion Bells............... 123
Looking Ahead.........   124
New March   125
First Step.................   126
Capricious.............   127
Last Rite   128
Take it easy...........   129
Defining Destiny........ 130
Finite Sphere 131
Validation   132
Conquerors...........   133
Off the Edge   134
Mission   135
Triumphant   136
Woven Reality.......... 137
The Pursuit   138
The Fact   139
Measure...............   140
Image in Eternity....   141
Seven Souls   142
Bottom-line........... . 143
Meditative Art......   144
Life...................   145
Unresolved..........   146
Against All   147
Being & Dignity 148
Nova Blueprint....... . 149
Our Time   150
Ascension.............   151
Path Ahead..........   152
Endeavor 153
Being & Time.......   154
Background........   155

Perplexed

Riding high
Through the dark
Clouds and waiting
For Sun to break

As we
Keep riding
The perplexity
Adventure; not
Knowing where
We may end up

While
Passing through
It all, let's grasp,
"What is
Being,
Substance and
Causation?"

That
Yet to be fully
Clarified, and
Still to rediscover,
"What is our real
Identity?"
In this set charade...

Be Calm

All we can
Say, "It's always a
New beginning," and
No time to procrastinate

Yes, it's
Just a renewal, and
Determination to
Conquer the mind only

Beware,
The trail is too
Long and plagued
By million unknowns
In between

Stay steady,
Be calm and
Be alert; steering
The mind toward
A path that is full of
Rhythms and meaning,
In its essence…

Recurrences

Somewhere
In time,
I am found and
Somewhere 'am
Lost

Sometimes,
I think, it's a
Mirage, and
Sometimes,
I believe there's a
Concrete meaning

So, in life,
I keep on
Spiraling between
Two extremes; known
And unknown, and
Still evolving

That is
The state of my
Curious mind, and
That is the state of my
Continued perplexity;
Keeping
My journey rolling…

The Way

We still
Need to clarify the
Significance,
"What is a pragmatic
Global justice?"

We still
Need a veritable
Middle Way to
Sustain a durable
Peace

In this context,
Hope must the
Destination of every
Struggling humans
For that be the every
New beginning

In other words,
Let's build a world of
Higher humanity and
Dignity; experiencing
Our full beauty and
Truth as the first step...

Existence 101

Not the
Punitive measures,
But the incentive step;
Bringing positive
Outcomes

That be the
Freedom from most
Evil consequences of
Human action

Not the
Constant flow of
Lies and deceptions
Of a given belief,

But a
Touch of
Compassion would
Free us

From
The "Built-in-guilt
Conscience" that's been
Imposed upon us
For a very long…

Reflection

I am a
Visible object of
The illuminated
Inner being called,
"The Soul"

That's why,
I understand,
Value of being
In harmony and
Peace and

That's why,
I must act morally
Through the integrity
Of my mind

Let it be my
Daily affirmation;
Enabling I to
Fearlessly keep
Walking through the
Light & the dark at
The same time...

Light & Shadow

All that I
Know, "We're
Shadows to the
Illumined
Inner being,

And existence
Seems, the
Battlefield of
Endless, "Rights
And wrongs"

Our precious
Time still under
The jaws of
Bigotry, violence's
And wars;
Undermining our
Moral possibilities

Why don't
We wake-up from
The long slumber and
Take charge, and be the
Shining light of all time!

Nova
Prayer

I am
Aware,
Therefore
I refuse to
Quit the
Scene

Yes, I am
Here to be
Awakened from
My deep sleep

Yes, I am
Here to
Overcome fear
And anxiety of
My time

Of course,
I am driven by
A big dream to
Fulfill my noble
Mission on time…

Endurance

Thought,
Reason and
Experience would
Complete my journey

Well, that's
Just half the story to
Win the totality of
My truth itself

Let
Meditative powers
Give lift and "I" fly
Off the half-opened
Cage in time"

It's only
Through such a
Mystical track;
Hoping to know,
"My moral meaning
With a full clarity,
All right."

Introspection

I am
No more than
What I think, dream
And aspired to be

In reality,
It's all about
My memories,
My experiences and
What I search for

I am
The sum total
Of an ephemeral
Point of view

I must exists
Only to pursue,
"Peace,
Harmony and
To keep alive

The Global Spirit,
"Humans are worthy of
Their births for they're
The perplexity, indeed."

Believe it

We're a
Spiritual
Continuum
And soar higher
Through any
Obstacle on the way

We're
Thunders and
Lightening of our
Creative thoughts,
Struggles and memories

And we keep
Rolling along this
Chaos, confusion and
Half-understood reality,
With some crazy whims

In such a
Nasty sand storm,
We're the blown-up
Fragmented grains;
Trying to settle down with
Calm and with some wisdom,
In return!

Inspiration

This being,
What a miracle
Consciousness

That's the
Only passage to
Realm of
The Unknown

That's the
Way to an
Anthrocosmic
Connectivity with
All that is

That's why,
This human though
A tiny speck
In the vast starry
Heavens

Still got
The courage to
Challenge the ultimate
Mystery, "Who he is and
What he ought to be?"

Our
Time

Rigid
Belief remains
In eternal conflict
With the moral
World

Objectivism
Too is in collision
Course against the
Endeavors to attain
A "Global Spirit" for
Peace

Even
Progressive liberals
And the conservatives
Too lose their identities
While bobbing into the
Sea of corruption

Well, the outcome
Isn't promising; forcing
Many millions to suffer
Through more than
It's necessary…

First Cause

We fall in
Love time after
Time and
Never knowing
What the end
Consequence would
Be

We can climb
The mountain high,
And we may get lost
In the misty
Early dawn,
And not knowing,
"Where're heading/?"

We hold
Our strong views
About life, laughter
And dream
Yet, we forget
To listen to others,
"What they're
Saying"

We wish
To change the world,
But we wait for others
To do it for us!

Image

What's left
In life is, but the
Memories to cherish

Of course,
It's all about,
What path
We've traveled from
Beginning to the
Nearing point

There
Once were caring
Parents and siblings,
Colleagues and good
Friends, but they're
All gone

There was
Once a validation
Being a successful
Professional in the world
And felt it was to be in the
Sunshine forever

Well, in no time,
We land simply into
The lapse of memories, and
Gone; we're merely, 'Urn"
And nothing more…"

Precious

Every being
Be the voice of
Conscience for the
Good of the whole

Only a few
Compassionate
Humans got the
Supreme capacity
To act accordingly

Let every being
Be the inventor of
Million ways to
Awaken the,
"Global Spirit of
Goodness "

Let love,
Bind all differences
And manifest into
One illumined humanity
And dare to go beyond

Let there
Be a miracle to
Us struggling beings, who
Never got to grasps their
Full-meaning at the core…

Forever

Dear
Sweet song of
My life:

It's your
Smile keeps me,
Rolling along the
Highway of
Happy dreams

Don't stop
Singing the love
Song for
That's the only
Essence to live for

Yes,
Dear sweet
Dream,
I adore your
Smile of deep
Feelings

I beg you,
To keep smiling
And singing that
Love song forever…

Sweetie

Glad to welcome
Parrot, "Sweetie"

She's charming
And full of alacrity;
Sustaining happiness
Every minute

From
Dawn to the dusk,
She keeps ringing the
World with harmony
And hope

Most of all,
She meditates for
A long and enjoys
Life even in her
Cage with so much
Love to live

Sweetie
What an amazing
Experience as we
Just began to know
Her calm and alert
State of mind simply…

Great
March

We
Shall prevail
We shall beat the
Odds and

We shall keep
The journey rolling
Toward the shining
Light

Let there
Be man-made
Rigid beliefs;
Opposing our
"Just Cause"

We don't
Give a damn for
We're
Marching along
A right path...

Queries

Mysteries of
Reality expressed
Through paradoxes,
Contradictions and
Riddles;

Sustaining
The half-evolved
Human; looking
An answer for
A very long

That's
Ever
Complexion
Of his state of
Mind, keeps
Evolving,
Life after life

In it all,
His existence
Seems one big
Never-ending puzzle
Yet happily keeping him
On the march forever...

Sinners

It's an
Insanity when a
Smoker thinks, "One
More won't kill me…"

It's a
Sheer lunacy,
When guardians think,
"We can trigger a war
And win it in no time"

It's a
Macho men's
Delusional hubris,
"I can get any girl,
I want"

It's a
Utter nonsense
When zealots claim,
"Their God is the
Greatest…"

That's
The bill board of
Evil minds;
Frozen in time…

Imitators

What if
AI's interprets
Truth being zero
And one, simply?

And, what if
We continue to
Believe all that fed by
The fancy machines?

In that case,
Is there any room left
To experience first-hand
Our freedom or what?

Tide of change;
Swiping away
All that we hold as
Mighty moral force

Who knows?
What if we end up
Worshipping,
"Techno-God" and
Ardently believing,
"Machine generated,
Truth!"

Revival

Let's
Rethink,
Human alone is the
Essence of existence

When
Intelligent beings
Grasp that authentic
Truth as such

They shall
Awakened to their
Inner will to win, and

That's how
Humans shall spark
Into this holistic web;

Discovering
Their own beauty and
Authenticity indeed...

Not
Singing

Folks are
Enquiring,
"Are we all trapped
Into some kind of
Hermetically sealed
Toxic box or what?"

Folks are
Even expressing
Their concern,
"Are we going to
Survive through this
Sinful world or not?"

Millions have
Lost good jobs that
Once earned bread with
A great pride and

Look at them,
Today; living in
Petite tents under
The super highways of
Their lost dreams…

Fortitude

We're
Sum of
All struggles
Put together
While evolving
From imperfection
To perfection

We're
Creatures of doubts
And debates born to
Know the right trail,
But we do go off the
Track, now and then

Each is
Alone, yet each is a
Part of the whole, and
Must bring right
Habits of the mind
On the scene

In the end,
We shall survive
Collectively only with
Moral fortitude as our
Solemn truth...

Amnesia

Heroes left
A plaque on one a
Virgin lunar terrain
That read:

"Here men from
The Planet Earth first
Set foot upon the Moon
July 1969 AD. We came
In peace for mankind."

It was one of the
Greatest turning points
As the world was
Simply mesmerized by
The novel adventure

Now space
Is a big biz venture
And with it,
We've ironically
Forgotten, deep
Meaning of that grand
Plaque right here on Earth,
Essentially…

Explorer

Human
Mind is a
Spinning sparks of
Consciousness;
Vibrating the mighty
Universe

It's the
Constant beam of
Mental thoughts; trying
To connect with all the
Mysteries of the holistic
Reality that we're trying
To comprehend

Human mind,
Charged with so much
Creative energy and a
Sincerity of a fearless
Will to win

Let him
Keep soaring higher
And higher till he hits the
Very meaning of the self
Through the set
Magnificent quest...

Cosmic Puzzle

Many
Universes
Exists and
Each got its own
Lyrics to sing

Some
Got intelligent
Life, perhaps

Others got
Life but
No intelligence
To brag

And some
Loaded with
Black holes and
Many unknowns

Truth seems
Incomprehensible to
Be grasped by our
Tiny three pound
Brains, perhaps!

When It Rains

When it
Heavily pours, it's
So windy and dark

And, folks keep
Running for shelter
Holding their fragile
Umbrellas, so tight

As if the
Entire humanity is
Desperately in a hurry
To get off the deluge

In such a
Dangerous place,
People quietly trying
To escape and

Sadly no where
To go but to wait out
The killer storm...

Being & Identity

What if,
Every being is
Standing on
The high
Pile of historic
Experience;
Seeking for
Truth today

Would it
Change their
World for good,
Or not with such
A noble mission, or
What?

What if,
Humans are
Ethical adventure,
Would they still lift
Humanity to the
High pedestal in their
Time or not...

Mission, "To be"

What we
Need is integrity
Of the mind

That is
The only way,
"Becoming"

Indeed,
That is the only
Passage, "What is
It all about?"

We're
Born to explore,
"What is immorality,
Soul or death …."

We're here
To grasp possibilities
Of our inner being
Well then
Why not conquer the
Mind and move on…

Leap of Self Faith

Human
Essence can't
Be reduced to an
Insignificance in this
Holistic reality

Yes, human
Alone is the only
Explorer who can dare
To resolve all riddles

That is
The authenticity
Of his supreme rational
Capacity backed by the
Moral will

Let him
Boldly probe the
Ultimate unknown;
No matter
Whatever the odds
There may be…

The Spirit

To be
In harmony with
All there is; must be
The best way to be
Free

It holds the
Mind at peace and
Let it focus on the
Challenges of
The age

In fact, that is
Where his fearless
Journey begins

Let him
Be driven by his
Incredible will

Let him
Keep
Walking along
The enlightened
Path and be free...

Epiphany

Nothing in
Life is impossible,
But your fear and
Anxiety; impacting
"Self-confidence"

It's necessary,
To be a disciplined
Mind and take the
Challenges with a
Daring self-belief

Only fearless and
Optimistic humans got
Better chance to win the
Lotteries, life after life

Let you
Be the center of the
Reality and
Let you call the shots
And let you never doubt
Your endless possibilities,
Albeit,
"That's what who you're."

Obsolescent

To convert
Either by force or
By fraud is a dying
Thing in this age of
Info all right

I mean,
Where
Billions believers
Can lucidly see its
Modus operandi
Through and through,
Today all right

That applies
To ideological push,
Over peddling of
Religious fervors or any
Insane fragmented claims

Folks all around
The world have awakened
And they know, "How the
Culprits play their losing old
Game…

Perfection

Mortal God
Who arrived to destroy
Evil and make room for
Good to assail must be
Worshipped

Mortal Human
Who exist for
Evil choices be dismissed
From the rational scene

Guardians
Making serious decision
Must honor wellbeing of
The whole get off the
Steering wheel

Lovers
Who fall in love must
Learn to wait for a long
Before saying, "We're in
Love forever"

Reformers
Who seek to change the
World must first change
Their conduct before
Declaring their
Intentions to the world…

Beware

Jingoistic
Human is an utter
Chaos to the whole

He's the
Violence and
Destruction of
All that is good

Be sure
To reform such
Odd balls; ensuring
Civil society to exists

Extremity
On any "Ism"
Brings nothing, but
Senseless blood spills

Let
Pious servants
And ambitious leaders
Take note:

"Humans seeks
A safe and just place
Where they can live…"

Juggernaut

We are
One collective
Intellectual
Enterprise

Each
Responsible to
Build a world of
Hope and harmony
For other

Let each
Comprehend the
Beauty of their
Own being

Let each,
Resolve conflicts
Within and keep the
Mojo going strong…

Road to Clarity

The prime
Object of human
Essence is to

Comprehend
Truth through the
Moral intention and
Deep rational insight

That is
How he shall
Experience first-hand
His authentic identity,
And be free

When he begins
To understand reality
With such an
Enlightened Third Eye

In fact, he shall
Intuitively be in grand
Unity of truth itself...

Scope & Limits

Our strict
Perceptuality
Takes
Us only half-way
Through while
Exploring the sum
Total of reality

Even,
Scientific
Endeavor
Too is limited to
Ford us half-way
Through

What is left
Is the power of
The "Intellectual
Mysticism;"

Let it
Open-up to the,
"Ultimate whatever"
And be the
Winner of his time…

Until Forever

Amid
Joy and sorrow
Keep dancing
Till the end of
Time

Yes, yes
Keep singing
The sweet song
Until forever

That's the
Vow,
We're taking
Today and

That's the
Truth of our
Love from this
Point on

Amid
Sickness and
Sorrow,
We shall
Be one mighty
Courage,
"Until forever…"

Be Bold

At this
Point, time
To stand tall
With a right cause

Time to
Erase hypocrisy,
Ignorance and
Intolerance from
The corrupt mind

Let
Our mighty
Moral will give us
Strength to meet the
Toughest challenge of
All time

Yes, time
To be bold;
Holding faith in
Ourselves to make
Impossible possible,
At this turning point…

Point Upward

Whenever a
Society sheds off
Thick layers of lies,
Bigotry and greed

There is a
Real celebration
Of humanity and
All rolls toward
"Good"

That is
Enlightenment,
That is
Genuine progress,
And that is the path
Called, "Truth"

Let us
Not fail,
Let us not quit
Let us
Be the moral will
To point upward…

Roll
The Balls

What if
We come together
And throw off the old
Vestiges, will it purify
Our hearts

Let's
Not accept the lie,
"We're doing well"
While ignoring;
Our demise at this
Time

Be aware,
Rampant corruption
And AI's are silently
Killing, "Who we're"

Let's
Act now
Before the said
Disease gets hold
Over our minds…

Gardener

Good
Emerges when
Positive attributes;
Self-confidence,
Humility and love
Are planted from
The beginning

In contrast,
Evil shows-up
In ignorance and
Indifferent attitude
Always

Either good or
Evil is
The consequence
Of the human mind,
Essentially

When
Each grasp such
A simple truth,
There shall bloom
Hope, Harmony and
Love in that inspiring
Garden...

Noble Warriors

We need
Strength to decipher
The complexities of
Reality
We've been in

It's our
Moral will and
Reason; permitting
To understand,
"Being Becoming"

We need
To grow-up soon
For we're drowning
Into the sea of fear
And anxiety on a large
Scale

Time
To adapt to new
Realities and time
To gather-up all
Strengths and rewrite
A new history,
"We're ready for our
Triumphs and truth."

Synergy

How do we
Arrive at
"Self-certainty"
In this reality of
Uncertainty?

Perhaps,
It's a mute issue
Of our time!

Perhaps,
It's an
Ignorance or
What?

We've
Devised different
Ways to tackle it
No answer yet

Perhaps,
If we combined,
Scientific with the
Mystic; that may
Shed some light…

Mystical Flow

Journey of
The spirit is nothing,
But a deeper
Understanding of the
"Self" and the world
Around it, I suppose

It's all about
Transcendence from
Self-conscious to the
Eternal consciousness

It's all about,
Knowing, "Where
We're and how do
We evolve from here
To eternity?"

And to that,
We call,
"Enlightenment,"
AKA
The rationale of
Our individual
Worthiness…

Being & Existence

Existence
Must be to
Conquer the
Corrupt mind,
Simply

That's the
First principle
To be
Validated before
Launching a long
Journey

Let
Existence be
Directed through
Freedom with
Equal
Responsibility

Let
Existence be
A live truth,

"How to restore
Our sanity from
Long list of blunders
And sins…"

Time Travelers

It's been
Known for eons,
"Introspection leads
In discovering our
Nature, what is a
Core essence…"

It's been
Told many times,
"The world is a
Manifest Good and
Should stay forever"

We're the
Live universe
Fired-up by infinite
Possibilities

So why not
Be fearless and
Change the world
For its own Good!

Will
To win

If we fail
To fulfill the
Set mission

We shall not
Return 'till the
Task is a success

If we fail
In love,
We shall never
Walk away from
The commitment,
We made

If life is
A biggest hurdle
To our dream
We shall
Fight all the way
Through to be
The heroes of our
Set mission…

Rise
Above

Let there
Be clarity,
Enabling us to
Reach the waiting
Goal?"

Let there be
No confusion,
"We're born to seize
Significance of our
Individual identity

Let us not
Blindly believe all
Lies and pseudo-claims
Imposed in our heads

Let us learn to
Honor
Our humanity and
Dignity with grace

Let us be
A moral force
And relearn, "How
To make right ethical
Judgments in the name of
All that is good"

Essence & Existence

Much
Intellectual dialogues
Is trapped by the
Linguistic complexity;
Leading to
Endless debates and
Subjective inferences

Great minds
Tried to address the
Challenge as stated yet
"Uncertainty" continues
To plague our attempt
For clarity

In such a
World of cause and
Consequence; where is
Certainty is a big issue
Still to be tackled

No, it's not
The dear divine, but
The very reality of human
Who's still twisting into
Changing state of the wind...

Connectivity

Self-
Consciousness
Is a source of
His eternal
Inspiration;

Leading, him
To know, "Who
'Am I and where I
Fit into this grand
Totality of whatever
It Is"

Oh yes,
This mystical
Being alone is the
Anthrocosmic
Connectivity

Let him glow
From nothing
To something in his
True essence, strictly

Journeymen

Our
Thoughts, words
And choices greatly
Defines,
"Who we're and what
We can become"

Our
Value judgment,
Commitment and a
Focus to the set
Goal shall lead us to
The illumined mind

Let's relearn
To think,
"We're larger
Than life always"

Let's take
Charge of life
And be the
Determined will
To win the journey
We've been on...

Great
Walk

Each living
Being is a logical
Projection of his
Perspective;

Emanating
His reason and
Experience built
Through time

That's how
He connects with
Others; witnessing
His own presence
In the world

While walking
Through the
Light and dark

He's caught
Between struggle and
Joy, love and hate and
Knows consequences
Of war and peace yet
Ignores 'em all, but why?

Being & Reality

In it all,
Human is the
Image of his
Reality

It's
Logical
Necessity,

To
The know,
"The Self in
Totality"

Human,
Defines value
Judgment and
Moral intention
To rise above his
Struggling plight…

Conundrum

Why
This finite
Being bounded by
A brief life, big dream
And unaware of his
Infinite possibilities,
Lost his,
"Self-confidence"

Is this a definite
Human with a
Moral will ready
To pick-up the gauntlet
And take a bold stand?

Is it a
New human
Who's the owner
Of his
Past, present and
Potential future
Or what?

"Why then,
He keeps
Stumbling over a
Smooth trail?"

In this
Age

Is the
Game of life,
About
Power, wealth and
Fame only or what?

Where do we
Draw the line
Between
Ego-centric
And Omni-loving
Journey of man

And, how do
We overcome the
Techno Guru AI's;
Intend to control the
Human mind

I mean,
How do we save:
Freedom, dignity,
Humanity from such
Negative forces of our
Time...

Falling
In Love

Young hearts,
Falling in love
Always

Young hearts,
Getting touch of
Grief and joy
While in love

Oh yes,
That's the
Nature of the beast
That's the greatest
Lesson to know it well

Remember,
Love is never a
Full guarantee, yet
It allows believing,
"It is"

Just enjoy the
Ride if you can while
Ignoring the consequences of
That magic called "Love."

Ascending Thrust

Meaning of
Every born human
Is his creativity

Along with it,
Morality to erase
Evil is a logical
Necessity to keep
In mind

That's the
Undergird reality,
"Being Becoming"

Let it be
The "Triumph of
The will" and

Let it be the
Mighty
Ascending thrust
Of inspiring hero of
The time…

Liberation

Being
May be a modicum
Drop into the paradoxical
Mode of existence

Yet must
Transits from illusion
To illumination; reshaping
His worldview in time

Let him
Be governed by his
"Own divine command"
And move on toward
Final liberation

Let him
Be a free will;
Streamlining his destiny
With the power of his
Core essence and let
Him just keep moving on…

A Point

"How human
Keeps embattling
At times through
Moral judging; thought
After thought, choice after
Choice; still looking for
A right track to walk"

What a
Continuum, "Cosmic
Dance;"teasing and
Ever testing his mettle
At every spin of the
Great Wheel

Oh yes,
Human always
A perplexing, evolving,
Exploding mind; caught
Into the milieu of some
Unknown Mirage!

Short
Falls

Let's see,
His moral
Commitment is a prime
Responsibility to ensure
Well-being of the whole,
But it's not happening

Though
He's a scintillating
Projection of all that is
Good; failing to meet
The measures of his
Ethical claims

Isn't it a
Perfect chance that
Every intelligent being
Strengthens his/her,
"Moral habit and acts
Accordingly just in time!"

Universal Human

Perhaps,
Reason is a full
Expression of human's
Supreme capability

Where
There is
No limit, but
The best possibilities
To soar higher and
Higher forever

Let him
Have such an
Audacity to be free
From the
Conceptual cage

Let it be the
Passage; transforming,
Him, "From ignorance to
An illumined mind as ever."

75

Odd Balls

In singularity,
Laws of physics
Don't apply

Yet reality
Persists and
Spikes-up with
Dark energy, super
Massive black holes and
Multiverses and so on

And
The Unknown Great
Wheel keeps spinning
From one mega yuga
To another, *ad infinitum*

In it all,
We're the cosmic
Odd balls,
Who've accidentally
Evolved for whatever
Purpose yet to be known

Now we're seeking,
"What's the meaning of
Invented God, reason and
Whatever may be in-between?"

As Ever

Keep dancing
With joy, but the
Joy only

Since our first
Cheek to cheek
Dance,

Dreams
Keep directing
The crazy feelings
Non-stopping

Tonight is
Another chance
To dance and

I say,
"Come,
Don't be afraid
For it's the dance
Of our destiny"

"Dear Heart,,
It's the journey until
We hit eternity through
Our love…"

First Principle

The Vedic
"Rit" is the first
Principle; challenging
"Divine Forgiveness"

As Rit boldly
Declares,
"Moral Justice
Stands above the
Divine agency"

That's why,
God Rama had
To obey the
Law of Rit and
Fight for justice
In his human form

Even the
Bhagavad-Gita
Had the same message,
"Those who don't obey
(Evil doers) must be
Brought to justice, even
The godly humans too."

Note
Well

Not
Religion, but the
Awakened being is
The moral force indeed

Not
Rituals and
Pseudo-claims
Of the zealots, but the
"Rational Goodwill" is
The real freedom to
Salute

Not the
False narratives of
The few super-greedy,
But the collective will
To lift humanity is the
Truth

Not the
Super smart AIs,
But the honor and dignity
Of human being is…

Illumined

Noble thoughts,
Words and actions
Greatly defines
Our journey to be

Let each
Human be creative,
Significant and
Persuasive

While
Rolling along the
Highway of many
Riddles, conflicts and
Perplexities

Let him
Keep walking
Steady along the
Enlightened trail

That is the
Direction of every
Committed calm and
Alert human to be...

Noble Journey

Doesn't
Matter at all,
What I think or
What I express via
Prose, poetica or
Whatever

It's just a
Worldview
Of an ordinary
Human only

Doesn't even
Matter what lyrics,
I write or sing 'em
Through feelings

'Am
Just another
Journeymen
Searching for his
Truth

That is
Simple as it
Should be while
I travel through
The given time…

Fearless

Being is
Born to be his
Own
Moral reason

For
That is the
Very essence,
"He's ever"

Never
Darkness force
Him to make evil
Choices

After all,
The set destiny
Must be a
Triumph of his
Magnifique quest

Let him
Stay focus and let
Him boldly keep the
Positive spirit flowing,
Forever…

Reckoning

Not religion,
But human is
The reality of
"Divinely moral
Duty call,
Sensu strictu"

Great minds
Kept reminding
Of such a simple
Truth time after
Time

And still,
Why bow down
To the old myopic
Narratives

Let's quit
The old habit and
Begin to steer toward
Our inner possibilities…

Perplexity

Oh yes,
Perplexity,
The mother of
All curiosities;
Thrusting every
Soul to know their
Truth

Human,
Always on the roll
To get to the
Perfection, and be the
Master of it all in
The end

Against million
Contradictions and
Lingering doubts and
Debates still he keeps
Steady along the
Track

Oh yes,
Fascination,
The mother of every
Walking being; keeping
Their best spirit in this
Mega charade all right...

Flush it Out...

Why
Listen to their
Dated crap

When they
Senselessly kill
In His good name

Why
Read their
Narratives when
They don't fit the
Modern time

Let
Reason and
Vision be larger
Than life

Why don't
They stand tall with
Love of humanity and

Work for a
Best future for their
Children in modern
World...

Reciprocity

What if
We invent a magical
Reciprocity between
Living and the dead

I mean,
Living here keeps
Committing evil
Acts and generating
A constant storm

While
The dead simply
Keeps purifying
Over there,
"Whatever that is?"

What if
Livings' sin is
Offset by the purified
Souls of the dead?

I mean,
Will it change the
World for good!

Wind of Change

In the
Old paper driven
World, half the time
Went in sorting out
The pile of info

Well, trash cans
Were happy then for they
Thought being important
In their masters productive
Life

Today,
It's all digital opium;
Keeping humans free from
The burden of paper stress

Hurray,
Something good has
Evolved and something
Big been lost as well

Yes,
No time left today
For a warm family
Conversations as humans
Have turned strangers...

Dice is Cast

Seems
The dice been
Cast and new pages of
History-in-making is
Already underway

Look at
The world around
Where poverty, despair
And ignorance remains
The prime narrative of
The time

We've
Miserably failed to
Build a peaceful and a
Safe world for children
At this very time

Each chapter
Essentially begins
With a deep concern,
"Near annihilation"

Nukes, climate,
Biogerms, AI's and
Greed ridden habit each
Can destroy the future...

Be
Alert

How do we
Tackle the issue of
Misfortune in this
Hedonistic world,
Today

Each is born
To ensure
Harmony and hope
To be alive from one
Generation to another

But then,
How do we restore
The sense of
Responsibility in
This ever challenging
Reality of today

Let's also ask,
"Why then we've
Succumbed to the false
Narrative bursting
With endless blunders
And sins?"

Moral Will

So much is
Talked and written
About
Humans and Nature

Is it not,
To rethink and
Act to resolve the
Issue of their
"Reconnection"

So much is
Preached and even
Imposed at times, but
That narrative hasn't
Worked well so far

Time
To be inspired
Through the fire of
"Moral Will" and

Take charge
Where humans
And Nature redefines,
"Harmony and hope…"

The Path

Let my
Path be the quest of
Clarity, order and
Gaining a futuristic
Vision while the
Ride is on

Let I
Be inspired by
The moral strength to
Redefine my waiting
Big dream today

Let, I
Pass through the
Existence called,
"Trials and Errors"
Of my slippery time

Let, I be
Rescued from the
Corrupt mind, and

Let, I be
Triumphant in all
Endeavors before
Death says, "Hello!"

The
Quest

A
Magnificent quest
Begins with a
Disciplined mind

So follow-up
Well with
Right thoughts,
Words and choices

Be sure
To know,
Each born human
Is a spiritual light

That is
Why nothing is
Impossible but the
Upward flight always

Be the
Positive minded
Hero of your mission
And give a meaning to
Your very worth…

Jet Stream

Life not
An ephemeral
Dream

It's a
Heroic journey
Of a determined
Mind

Life not
A disorder, but
A silent order of
Every awakened
Being

It's all
Either one big
Distortion or a well
Designed blueprint
Of the mind

Don't give-up
And run away from
The Enlightened
Spirit for your time is
Here and now only…

Arrows In-flight

Intelligent
Humans are
Arrows in flight

Sometimes
They flow toward
Right direction and
Sometimes, they don't

That is
The nature of brutal
Existence and that is
The world we're
Locked-in

Where
Certainty and
Uncertainty keep-on
Colliding at the same
Time and all remains
In imbalance

That's why,
"Learn how to
Steer through million
Patches of unknowns"
While being in the flight...

Outcome

In solitude,
We become
Bold and aware
Of the self

In harmony,
We become humble
And willing to accept
Others being equal

In hope,
We keep evolving
Along a same trail

In love,
We experience
Same consequence:
Either grief or joy

In truth,
We're lost, if we
Don't sharpen our wit
And being moral…

Not Quite

A leap
From cave
Dwellers to
The modern
Techno-Human,
Indeed is a big
Miracle itself

In between,
Myriad bumps
On the way, but our
Kind triumphant
At every turning point

Once when
Nature was
Worshipped with
Intense sincerity and
For spiritual purpose,
"We knew we're
Humans all right"

And when
Evil doers entered
The scene, they robbed
Our humanity, at once as
History is our best witness…

I, Dare

I've
No complaint to
Report,
I've
No compliment
To offer either

Let "I"
Keep probing
My meaning,
I mean, "Where
Can I experience
My Truth"

No point
In swinging back
An forth; signifying
Nothing while the
Trial is on

Let I
Meet face to face,
"My image in the
Mirror of all riddles;
Conquering my Truth…"

Unsettled

It's been an
Uneasy relationship
Between God and the
Undisciplined humans

Almighty
Demanding,
"To obey His Will,"
But the ignorant can't
Get off their hedonistic
Mesmerized magic

While Divine
Wants good to rule,
But the believers,
Not knowing, "What's
The meaning of good?"

That is
State of the unsettled
"Almighty," in this
Age of the lost humans…

Biggest Gamble

Yes,
Lovers are
Crazy all right
Who often
Falls in love so
Unexpectedly

Well love is a
Long struggle to
Build a strong and
A sweet relation
Between two souls

There is
Series of trials,
Tribulations and even
Shattering of dreams
Before two hearts
Become one

Of course,
Lovers always
Jumping onto a
Lane; sometimes
They're full of joy
And sometimes,
They're not…

Epicenter

At the
End of the day,
"Human is the
Destiny"

He is the
Eternal glow of
Inspiration to be

Albeit a
Builder of
Self-confidence
And fight all the
Unknowns

Again,
In the
Final analysis,
It's human, "Who's
The ultimate…"

Happy Morons

What if we're
The modern day,
"Techno-happy
Morons"

Who've
Forgotten,
"Who they're
And giving way to
Their noble goals
To the non-human
Machines?"

What if we're
Lazy humans
Whose undergoing
Amnesia of our real
Identity may be?

What we're
Yesterday and what
We've become today
Is something to be
Reckoned soon?

Closing Curtain

As time
Nears to say,
"Goodbye," all seems
Fading fast from
The Soul itself

Yes, the
World once my
Dearly held dream,
Now is heading
Toward another
Unknown

Now, solitude is
My reliable pal;
Driven by a few good
Memories popping-up,
Now and then

I am moving away
From yesterday as I
Near the unknown
Tomorrow

Let it be
A new dawn, a new
Enlightened journey,
To say, "Hello" again…

Flickers

Life
When
Contemplated
Retro-perceptively,
Seems like a flash

Indeed,
All, simply is
Fleeting events and
Nothing to hold on
For a long

Love-hate,
Right-wrong,
Grief and joy,
Hope-despair simply
Goes off the scene

Death
Calls them,
"Just bubbles
At the surface," and
Nothing more while
I live through my
Allocated time here…

Rhythms

Love shall
Ride us from one
Heaven to another,
Always

Love shall
Give us meaning
From one life to
Another for sure

I ask,
"Why don't you
Understand the depth
Of our feelings"

Yes, dear
I insist, let's begin the
Grand venture today,
And be meaningful
While the journey's on

Come, let us
Launch
The sweet adventure
Of this eternal love and
Be in harmony with our
Souls forever, forever...

Mistaken Identity!

Only a
Handful minds
Changed the
Way we know the
World we're in

They're
Real heroes in
Every age
Everywhere, but
We fail to remember
Them when the
Call is for us to act

They're
The Global Spirits
Looking far above the
Fragmented mindsets

Sadly,
Their voices are
Being buried by the
New techno-narratives
And the false beliefs and
Fickle opinions…

Being & Purpose

Time has
Arrived and I stand
Alone before this
Great Void" called,
"My Unknown"

While
In the world, I tried
To know things
Well with new
Vigor, new ways
To think and

Of course
Whatever petite
Moral intention,
I could muster

Like any other,
I seek to live in the
World of understanding,
Tolerance and adaptability
In the name of
Good essentially...

A Spin

It was all once
Many attachments:
Family, friends,
Endless wonders and
Many million dreams

In time
They slowly began
To fade as the
Body turned frail and
The mind began thinking
Something else

Eventually,
Body, mind and
Reality …all closing
Circle left behind, and

Only
The Magic Spark
Remains to the end and
Nothing else and that is in
Short, the grand saga of
Every being…

Line in
The Sand

What is the
Meaning of anything
When nothingness is the
Ultimate to greet

What is the
Purpose of being moral
When the world is in the
Grips of everyday evil
In full-action

What is the
Significance of a belief,
If it is driven by vengeance,
Violence and cruelty in
The name of what is
Still Unknown

What is the
Justification of inventing
Super smart-thinking
Machines, if the ultimate
Objective is to control
The human minds…

Return
To Source

Where once
I was a
Part of true humanity
Where moral harmony
Cemented simple folks of
The time

It was
In that small town
Where everybody knew
Everybody

As they
Met daily in temples
Market places and
At every happy event

World then was
Only horse carriages,
Bicycles and lots of
Heat and dust, but the
Real freedom was there…

We're Masters

Time is
In the mind
Otherwise, we're in
Eternity always

Divine
Too is in the mind,
Otherwise, we
Can be in solitude
Always

We're
In-charge of our
Thoughts, conduct and
Choices;

Defining the
Future course of
Our waiting dream

We're the
Ultimate determinant
Either to be happy
Or be in despair and

That's how
We're the masters of
Oure imperfect existence...

Blind Logic!

If
Two children
Stole couple
Cookies
From the jar,

How do
We label,
All children of
The world
To be thieves?

If two
Humans eat the
Sweet fruit from
Someone's farm,

How do
We brand
Entire humanity,
Be guilty of such
A petite sin?

Why promote
Such a notion
When humans are
Children of only one
Loving Unknown!

Smart Idiots

It's very funny,
Even we feel highly
Spirited yet we're
Going nowhere

All meanings
Keep spinning into
Three pound machine,
But no real awakening
To experience

And many of
These "Smart idiots"
Affirms,

"They got all
Answers to ills of the
Suffering society,"

Yet the world's
Keeps bleeding
With violence, death and
Destructions, and there is
No deep concern...

Here & Now

When
Equality of men
Women is locked-in
In the promises,
No wonder,
"The issue remains
Unsettled""

When
A religion
Holds, "Peace and
Compassion and
Fails merciful One,"
How long will it
Control the minds

Why're
The leaders hiding
From the urgent scene?

Why're
The reformers
So silent in this dire
Time!

Gear-up

Only
Introspection
Lead us from
Disorder to order,
At once

Only
Moral endeavor
Lifts humanity
To all possibilities
In the end

Don't
Shut the mind
Out of
Anxiety and fear

Don't shut
The eyes from
Seeing the world
Of greater worth

Don't just
Stand there;
Ruminating with
Regrets and guilt

Be brave,
Gear-up and walk
The walk …

Perfunctory

People
Feeling alone
Though
Being with many
Million others

People
Doing things
With no heart in it,
Still keep spinning into
Their closed circle

Endless chores
Impacting the
Over-occupied
Existence; denying
Beautiful moments of
Reflection and harmony

Lately, these
AIs, smart phones…
Smart TVs; stealing
Their precious time…

Keep Walking

Nothing
Better than
Freewill to unveil
The unknown

Nothing
Greater than the
Rational goodwill

Cycles of
Life never-ending
Grief and joy and

Let each
Navigate
Through it all
In calm and alert

That's the
Best passage
To make it all the
Way to the temple
Of set goals.

Through Time

Why
Be perplexed of
Our existence,

"When we're the
Cause of
Its imperfection"

Why
Be in the state of
Denial?

"When
We've failed
To know our real
Possibilities and hope"

Let's
Get it right, we're
Historic blunders,
And we need to change
Our basic nature,
As soon as we must…

Let's
Fly off

Come let's
Fly off the edge
And enjoy soaring
Beauty of all that is
In the endless skies

Let's leave
The noise behind
And experience this
Magnifique Nature
With an open mind

Let's just
Keep flying over the
Endlessness called,
"All that is"

Come,
Let's correct the
World that's still
Under the spell of
The seven sin…

An Epic

We're
An intelligent life
Sailing through
Blessed eternity

But we're
Caught between,
"Unity and Division"
Of subjective beliefs

Though
In essence
We're equal Souls
From the same
"World Soul,"

Sadly,
We keep killing
Each other; I mean
So senselessly

What a pity,
We've not yet
Understood, "How to
Live in harmony and
Peace, at least for the
Good of our kids…"

Dots of Reality

We're
The intelligent dots
Eventually shall fade
Away as there is no
Guarantee, we shall
Be ever again

While being
On the journey of
Our collective meaning,
"Why not relearn, how
To see each other being
Friends and not strangers"

Let us
Explore this
Fascinating reality
With whatever wisdom
We can muster today

And let's
Get to some logical
Conclusion,
"We're the holy images
In the final analysis…"

Being & Journey

Every
Sentient must
Seek solitude from
The maddened
World

Every
Illumined
Mind must seek
Answer to their
Inner persona
To be free

Being alone
Is the extension
Of a cosmic magic

Let him
Celebrate,
"He's born to bring
Sanity to his turbulent
World simply"

Life-force

To each a
Place to think,
To reflect and to
Vision the major
Task ahead

Let each
Beautify rhythm,
Melody and meaning,
"What's the original
Purpose after all?"

Let each
Stand firm on the
Sacred truth and be
The reformer to build
A better world

Let each
Get ready and go
To the destiny called,
"Happiness to the whole."

Clarion
Bells

Heaven is
Far away and
Still time to wait

Meanwhile,
Humanity here is
Plagued by the
Disease, danger and
Rampant greed

There is
Neither vigor nor
Will to escape from
The chaotic cage since
Human is locked-in for a
Long

Clarion bells
Are ringing
Everywhere, but
The intelligent mind
Still snoring into the
Deep slumber...

Looking Ahead

Mind
Eternally
Caught between
Life & death,
Chaos & order,
Reality & uncertainty
And whatever else

What's
The value of any
Belief which offers
Division and falsity to
Retain myopic mind-set

Time to
Grow-up and see
The big picture before
Humanity is no more…

New
March

Pawns
We're of the
World of sheer
Ignorance

Patients
We're where
Each suffering
One way or other

Nowhere
To go from the
Hellish state of the
Mind where violence
And death seems writing,
The epitaph

Come,
Let's begin a new
March for clarity
And be better us...

First Step

"I," a
"Universal Spirit"
Born to be larger
Than life

"I" a
Turning point;
Passing from
Impossible to
Possible

"I,"
Just an ordinary
"Determined will"
Keeps probing,
"All that is"

"I," striving
To evolve from
Shaky beginning
To a firm moral
Fortitude, only…

Capricious

Why
Folks go crazy
While in love

Why do
They switch from
Good to evil when
Things run well

Love,
What a beauty and
Despair at the same
Time

Why
Folks keep screaming,
Fighting and being
Nasty

While
Flying through
The awesome beauty
Of love!

Last Rite

From above,
I see my body laid
To be viewed at the
Morgue

A few
Who cared, gave
Their precious time;
Bringing beautiful
Flowers along

Some eulogized
With utmost love;
Expressing good
Memories to share

Then the priest
Sprinkled Holy water
Over the body at sleep
And recited some quotes
From the
"Enlightened Book"

Soon, coffin was
Cremated; leaving just
A few ounces of urn; ending
"All That I was once…"

Take it Easy

While
Walking through
Desire, dream and
High ambition

Be sure to
Self-restrained,
And be calm and
Alert at all time

Remember,
One day all that
You cared and love
Shall come to an end;
Sometimes abruptly
Too!

Treat today
Being the last day,
And keep focused on the
Goal to be simple and
Good in the name
Of humanity you d care…

Defining, Destiny

We mustn't
Be perplexed
Whenever
Existence turns
Rudderless

But we must be
Concern when
Human ignores his,
"Inner persona" for
Whatever reason

Let him know,
Life is brief and
The journey too long
Yet rewarding, so
Get smart soon

That's the
Only way to
The realm of
Meaning, beauty and
Truth and be worthy of
His time…

Finite
Sphere

**There is a
Point where one
Mustn't freeze in
Time**

**There is a
Life where
Every human
Must define
Destiny in time**

**There is
Love in the
World that be
Powered by trust**

**There is
Good friendship,
To be nourished
By its deep meaning**

**There is a
Way to live well,
It's called,
"To be simple and a
Caring human as ever."**

Validation

Monumental
Grandeur be
Dedicated to the
Sons and daughters
Of the world

"Who
Fought for the
Good of humanity
In their times"

I mean,
Let us offer our
Deep gratitude to 'em
For morally inspiring
Through the time

Let us
Celebrate their
Collective sacrifices
In the name of
Strengthening our,
"Global spirit" that
Yet to be bloomed…

Conquerors

"Why life is
So significant, and
Yet there is still the
Lingering darkness?"

Why not
Conqueror the
Mind; bringing
Light to every
Joy to live well

Time
To be aware of
Our collective
Glories and blunders,
And begin a new
Journey at this time

Let us
Dare to be
Conquerors, and
And vividly know,

"What's our
Human essence in this
Rapidly changing world…"

Off
The Edge

As if
My soul is distancing
Away from where
I was born, grew-up
And began the tough
Journey for decades

In-between,
Being blessed with
Infinite parental and
Sibling's love

Then I married
To a magnificent
Girl; showing me,
"What true love ought
To be through time"

Two wonderful
Children gave deeper
Meaning to my life and a
Few friends who understood
Value of friendship well

I am grateful
To everyone, but it's
Time to say, "Goodbye"
As eternity is waiting for
My return at this time…

Mission

We're
History of ideas
And curiosities still
To be fulfilled

Of course,
We're here
To understand:

Paradoxes,
Contradictions and
Mysteries that are
Endless to be grasped

For
Millennia, we're
A bold adventure to
Unfold, "What is the
Meaning of our own
Being in the world?"

Let's begin
With a single aim,
"What is our truth
In this fascinating
Realm called, *Life full
Of great riddles*?"

Triumphant

What's
This craze of
Promoting one
Myopic narrative,
In this twenty-one?

Why not
Explore the
Moral core of
Humanity with a
Larger perspective
Of what is,"Good"

Even
We can probe,
"What we ought to be
And how to be going
Beyond"

Let us
Be a determined
Force called, "Truth"
And let us
Complete the journey,
At this turning point.

Woven Reality

All that
We know seems
Perpetual motion;
Transcending from
Imperfection to
Perfection

Human
Is no exception,
Whence keeps
Ascending from
Darkness to
Illumination

All that we
Experience is
Witnessing nothing
But a universal flux

Concomitantly,
Everything is going
From cocoon to the
Flying freewill's into
This exploding Universe…

The
Pursuit

Vedic
Thought insisted,
"Our direct
Experience is not of
Apparent reality, but
Something far more
Deeper and beyond…"

Even
Modern scientists
Are in agreement with
Such a conclusion as
Revealed
By the quantum
Thinking

Let the mind
Evolve higher and
Let the meaning of
Our mega-curiosity be
Resolved, ultimately,
Via regia
"Total intuitive
Mysticism…"

The Fact

Death is
Essentially a noble
Passage to eternity

That's why
One shouldn't be
Fearful of it at all

Birth is
Definitely joy to
The world yet it must
Walk through other-half
Called, "Grief"

Love,
What a thrill
Between two waiting
Hearts, yet at times, the
Beast be governed well

Truth,
What an inspiring
Gift yet it can be a
Teasing mirage; driving
One from peace to a
Destructive being as well!

Measure

To withstand
Adversity with grace
And clam is the hallmark
Of an enlightened mind

To be fearless
Means to take a
Moral stand without
Concerned to the
Consequences

Only
An awakened
Soul is able to grasp,
Significance of
Essence and existence,
While walking through
The rough terrain

In illusive world,
All opinions are merely
Blurred images projected
On a mega-screen where they
Turn irrelevant time after
Time …

Image
In Eternity

I contemplate
My total reality
While walking along
This unknown trail

I know,
My times brief,
Million ambitions
To be fulfilled

Not afraid
To walk alone
To know my truth,
But I got to discipline
The monkey mind

In the end,
"I am," only an
Image in eternity;
A tiny spark of
Consciousness; seeking
"What I ought to be."

Seven Souls

I still remember,
The seven caring
Souls with whom
I walked for a while

Yes,
They vibrated
My heart and mind
Like the seven
Melodious strings

Now,
They remain a
Flow of inspiration;
Revolving in the
Mind, time after time

Each soul
Struggled to reach
The ultimate triumph
And each left a great
Legacy, "How to be a
Good human being…"

Bottomline

Truth
Is an open
Big game,

Anyone
Can enter its
Arena to probe,
To know, to
Understand; even
Seize its beauty
On the spot

Truth,
Must be free
From "Mental
Conceptuality"

Truth,
Where chaos
And order, clarity
And confusion and
Subjectivity and
Objectivity; losing
Their meaning...

Meditative Art

Intrigue
Is the great
Art creation

Where
Viewers are
Mesmerized by
It's abstractive
Depiction

Look at
The mysterious
Smurf of
"Mona Lisa, or
The Scream" of
Edward Munch

What
Wonderful feelings
They stir up in every,
Silent soul…

Life

Life is a
Continuum
Laughter's and
Tears, all we
Know

Life is
To enjoy its
Beauty and truth,
Also

Life is
A big question,
"Why we keep
Spinning through
Birth and death?"

Life,
What a last
Chance to probe,
"Who we're and
What's the
Meaning of it all?"

Unresolved

We humans,
Define our
Ordinary reality

That's
Driven
By the past,
The present and
Still to embrace
The future ahead

We're either
A mirage or a
Concrete experience
To believe or to be
Ignored while
The ride is on

Our
Conceptuality
Seems
A nasty riddle,
And we're thickly
Striving to be
Understood still!

Against Odds

After
Innocent
Birth,
In time human
Evolves from

Simplicity to
Complexity and
Then all bets are
Off

That is the
Non-stop
Conveyer belt,
Life after life

Only way
Out is to
Have a pure
Courage and

Conquer
Higher dimensions
Of thoughts packed
With moral intentions.

Being & Dignity

It's not
What I imagined
To be, but how I make it
Through it all with some
Detachment and calm

In this
Chameleon drama,
I got to be,
"Self-awareness"
At every
Turning point

While
Inching through
Endless trials, errors
And blunders of this
Fragmented subjective
Beliefs

I got to be
Ready to defend my
Dignity, My humanity.
My precious reality,
At all time…

Nova Blueprint

Well,
We know,
Modern society shall
Keep changing in
Response to myriad
Forces either positive
Or otherwise, but mostly
Both

Against
Such a backdrop,
"Do we still understand?
We too have to change;
Erasing old
Habits: violence, wars
And distrust…"

The main issue
Then "Is there a
Way to rewrite another
Blueprint of our collective
Future at this critical
Time or not!"

Our
Time

Being born
Into the complex
Spider-web of endless
Analysis, synthesis, dualism,
Dialectics and more

Seems
We've been drowning
Into the restless stormy
Sea of mental gymnastics,
All right

Again, we keep
Bobbing into such a
Turbulent scene with
Burdening subjectivity vs
Objectivity, theists' vs
Atheists and many more
Such, "Half-and-Half"

Oh yes,
We've been dancing
All along crazy whims;
Sustaining the chaotic
Harmony, all right…

Ascension

A life with a
Purpose is always
Greater than one
Without

That's the
Very spirit driven
By those heroes with
Optimism and an
Open mind;

Letting us pass
Through the troubled
Waters and rejuvating
Our spirit each time

Let us
Rejoice and celebrate
Their collective
Strengths;

Inspiring
Us to soar up
From darkness to the
Ever brighter light...

Path
Ahead

Like
A phoenix,
Time to wake-up
From the darkness
Left behind

And relearn,
How to
Shine with a new
Vigor, new vision and
A new harmony in
Our time

Let's
Open our minds;
Rekindling,

"How do we
Complete the noble
Mission; leaving a
Legacy of happiness
Behind to the young…"

Endeavor

Destination,
Reconnection is the
Way to our long pursuit
Of Truth

That's the
Bold journey, we've
Been on for some times

Isn't it time
To be reflective
And enjoy the very
Beauty what is today

And,
Get ready for
A perfect
Many tomorrows
Let's keep-up
The zeal

Come, let's be
Reconnected being
Moral humans and
Truly be free…

Being & Time

They thought,
World is essentially
An empirical reality;
Dismissing
Anything beyond

Then there
Were the linguistic
Judges tried to ignore
Poetica and metaphysics;
Frankly dismissing
Them "Meaningless"

When arrogance
Slams the world of
Metaphysical queries;
Only ignorance remain
Sovereign

Today,
Cosmic adventures
And quantum thinking is
Changing our notions about
The big bang and so on, and
Seems we're heading
Toward metaphysical either
Directly or indirectly all right.

JAGDISH J. BHATT, PhD
Brings 45 years of academic experience including a post-doctorate research scientist at Stanford University, CA. His total career publications: scientific, educational and literary is 100 including about 60 books.